PUFFIN BOOKS

PIRATE PENGUINS AND
THE NOSTRILS OF NEPTUNE

Frank Rodgers has written and illustrated a wide range of books for children: picture books, story books, non-fiction and novels. His children's stories have been broadcast on radio and TV, and a sitcom series based on his book *The Intergalactic Kitchen* was created for CBBC. His recent work for Puffin includes the swashbuckling Pirate Penguins series, and new titles in the bestselling Witch's Dog series. Frank was an art teacher before becoming an author and illustrator, and he lives in Glasgow with his wife. He has two grown-up children.

D0347788

Books by Frank Rodgers

PIRATE PENGUINS

PIRATE PENGUINS AND THE
SARDINES OF DOOM

PIRATE PENGUINS AND THE
NOSTRILS OF NEPTUNE

THE WITCH'S DOG

THE WITCH'S DOG AT THE
SCHOOL OF SPELLS

THE WITCH'S DOG AND THE
MAGIC CAKE

THE WITCH'S DOG AND THE
CRYSTAL BALL

THE WITCH'S DOG AND THE
FLYING CARPET

THE WITCH'S DOG AND THE
ICE-CREAM WIZARD

THE WITCH'S DOG AND THE
BOX OF TRICKS

THE WITCH'S DOG AND THE
TALKING PICTURE

THE WITCH'S DOG AND THE
TREASURE MAP

THE ROBODOG

THE ROBODOG AND THE BIG DIG

THE BUNK-BED BUS

Frank Rodgers

Pirate Penguins and the Nostrils of Neptune

PUFFIN

To every whale in every sea – swim free

PUFFIN BOOKS

Published by the Penguin Group
Penguin Books Ltd, 80 Strand, London WC2R 0RL, England
Penguin Group (USA) Inc., 375 Hudson Street, New York, New York 10014, USA
Penguin Group (Canada), 90 Eglinton Avenue East, Suite 700, Toronto, Ontario, Canada M4P 2Y3
(a division of Pearson Penguin Canada Inc.)
Penguin Ireland, 25 St Stephen's Green, Dublin 2, Ireland (a division of Penguin Books Ltd)
Penguin Group (Australia), 250 Camberwell Road, Camberwell, Victoria 3124, Australia
(a division of Pearson Australia Group Pty Ltd)
Penguin Books India Pvt Ltd, 11 Community Centre, Panchsheel Park, New Delhi – 110 017, India
Penguin Group (NZ), 67 Apollo Drive, Rosedale, North Shore 0632, New Zealand
(a division of Pearson New Zealand Ltd)
Penguin Books (South Africa) (Pty) Ltd, 24 Sturdee Avenue, Rosebank, Johannesburg 2196,
South Africa

Penguin Books Ltd, Registered Offices: 80 Strand, London WC2R 0RL, England

puffinbooks.com

First published 2008
1

Set in Times New Roman Schoolbook
Made and printed in Singapore by Star Standard

British Library Cataloguing in Publication Data
A CIP catalogue record for this book is available from the British Library

ISBN: 978–0–141–32288–9

I t was spring-cleaning time aboard the iceberg ship, the *Frozen Kipper*.

Paisley, the captain, was tidying his cabin . . .

Spott, the lookout,
was sweeping out
the crow's-nest . . .

Posso, the first
mate, was
ironing the
skull and
crossbones . . .

And Kelty,
the cook,
was cleaning
the stove.

"Look what I've found!" cried Paisley,
hurrying on to the deck.
He waved an old piece of
parchment in the air.

"It's signed by my Grandpa Elgin . . .
the very first pirate penguin. Come
and see what he's written.
It's exciting!"

The crew gathered round as Paisley
pinned the parchment to the mast.

Search for Neptune
Where the Ice Wind blows
My treasure lies hidden
Right under his nose.
signed Elgin

"When I was a little penguin, Grandpa
Elgin told me he had hidden some
treasure. This must be it!" exclaimed
Paisley with a wide grin.
"Isn't that
wonderful?
We must go
and look for it."

"But what about Neptune?" asked
Posso uneasily. "He's the King of the
Sea, isn't he?

Maybe he
won't want
to give up
the treasure."

"And not only that," said Spott,
"but the Ice Wind is the wildest wind
in the north."

"Yes," added
Kelty. "It can
blow you right
out of your
socks."

Paisley looked at his crew. "You're
not scared, are you?" he asked.

"Er . . . of course not," they replied.
"Well then," said Paisley with a grin,
"what are we waiting for? Let's go!"

Chapter Two

"Grandpa's treasure, here I come!" sang Paisley loudly as they sailed north.

The crew covered their ears. "What a terrible noise!" complained Posso.

"I know," replied Paisley cheerfully.
"I'm not a good singer. But
Grandpa was. And he was a
wonderful musician.

When he played his concertina even
the whales began to sing."

"I've never heard whales
singing," said Posso.
"But I'd like to."

"Me too," added Kelty. "Any kind
of singing as long as it's not
Paisley's!"

Paisley laughed. Then suddenly,
without any warning, a cold wind
shrieked across the deck. The flags
flapped and snapped, and the sails
strained against the ropes.

"The Ice Wind!" cried Paisley above
the howling gale.
"Take care,
everyone!"

Posso quickly tied
himself to the ship's wheel
as Kelty darted
into the safety of
the galley kitchen.

Gripping tightly on to a rope,
Paisley looked up and gasped.

The Ice Wind had taken Spott by
surprise. He had been blown out of
the crow's-nest and was now
hanging on by his flipper-tips.

"Hold on, Spott!"
shouted Paisley.
"I'm coming!"

Fighting against the wind, Paisley
bravely pulled himself up the
swaying rigging.

It was very hard, but at last he reached
the crow's-nest and climbed in.
Spott was flapping helplessly about
like a piece of washing on a line.

Leaning out into the gale, Paisley
grabbed hold of Spott's flippers.

"One, two, three . . . pull!" he shouted
and, with a mighty heave, hauled
Spott back into the crow's-nest.

"Thank you, Paisley," gasped Spott.

"Not at all," said Paisley. "Just make sure you get back down to the deck all right."

"I will!" replied Spott. Carefully, he climbed back down the rigging, holding on as tightly as he could.

Once Spott was safely on deck,
Paisley began to climb down.

But, halfway
down, the Ice
Wind got
much stronger.
With a nasty
howl it hurled
itself across
the sky.

Paisley's flippers
slipped from
the ropes.

In an instant, the screaming wind
plucked him from the rigging and
tossed him into the air.

"Help!" yelled Paisley. "Let me
down!"
But the wind just blew him higher
and higher instead.

Down below on the *Frozen Kipper*,
Posso, Kelty and Spott watched in
alarm as their captain soared into
the clouds . . .

and disappeared from sight.

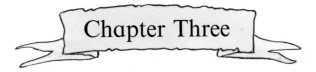

Chapter Three

When the wind dropped at last, the crew of the *Frozen Kipper* sprang into action.

Kelty set the sails while Posso spun the wheel, turning the *Frozen Kipper* in the direction that Paisley had disappeared.

The iceberg ship raced over the
waves. From the crow's-nest, Spott
scanned the sea with his telescope.

"I can't see him!"
he called down.
"I hope he's all
right."

"I hope so too,"
said Posso
anxiously.

"And me,"
added
Kelty.

On and on the *Frozen Kipper* sailed,
and still Spott searched the ocean.

"See anything
yet?" asked
Posso hopefully.

Spott shook his head. "No – " he
began, then stopped.

"Wait a moment,"
he said. "I do
see something."

"Is it Paisley?" asked Posso excitedly.

Spott sighed and shook his head again.
"No," he replied sadly. "It's only a whale." Then all of a sudden his eyes lit up and he laughed in delight.

"But Paisley's there too! He's riding on the whale's back!"

Spott, Kelty and Posso gathered at the side of the ship and watched, grinning, as Paisley and the whale came alongside.

Paisley waved cheerily.

"This is Murkle," he said, patting the whale. "The Ice Wind dropped me into the sea right next to him and he rescued me."

"Thank you for saving our captain," said Posso.

"A pleasure," Murkle replied in a slow, low, gurgly sort of voice.

Just then three other whales surfaced beside Murkle.

"These are Murkle's friends . . .
Troon, Mull and Pladda," said
Paisley.

"And guess what? They're heading
towards their feeding grounds beside
an island called Neptune."

"Neptune? That must be what your
grandpa was talking about, Paisley!"
said Posso with relief.

"Not the
actual
King of
the Sea."

"I'm sure it is," replied Paisley with a
smile. "And Murkle and his friends
are going to lead us there."
He patted the whale again.
"Is there anything
we can do for
you, Murkle?"
he asked.

Murkle blinked slowly. "There are lots of whale hunters about these days," he said. "Would you warn us if you see any?"

"We certainly will," answered Paisley, climbing aboard the *Frozen Kipper*.

"Don't worry, Murkle. We'll keep you safe. That's a promise."

Chapter Four

As the *Frozen Kipper* followed the whales north, Spott kept a sharp lookout for whale hunters.

"The Ice Wind's blowing again," said Posso. "But thankfully it's not too strong."

"It's strong enough to take us speedily to Grandpa's treasure, though," said Paisley with a laugh.

"Land ho!" called Spott at that
moment. "Neptune!"
Up ahead, a craggy island appeared
out of the mist.

"No wonder it's called Neptune,"
said Paisley. "Look . . . the
mountain is shaped just like the
King of the Sea."

"Yes . . . there's his crown," said Posso.

"And there's his face," added Kelty.

"And there's his nose!" cried Paisley happily. "My grandpa's treasure should be hidden right under it!"

As the *Frozen Kipper* sailed into a
narrow bay, the huge, rocky nose
loomed high above them.

Looking up at the
nose, Paisley laughed
out loud when he saw
that he was staring
into the openings of
two dark caves.
"Hah!" he cried.
"The nostrils of
Neptune!"

Posso laughed too.
"Let's hope he doesn't
sneeze," he said.

But that's exactly what happened.
The wind picked up and the crew of
the *Frozen Kipper* heard a rumbling
sound deep inside the mountain.

A few moments later there was a
great whooshing sound, and twin
blasts of wind and spray shot out
of the caves.

SSSCHOO!

The pirate penguins were bowled over like skittles and rolled across the deck.

Paisley grinned ruefully as he picked himself up. "Neptune probably does that a lot," he said.

"But next time we'll be prepared."

They quickly tied
the *Frozen Kipper*
to a large rock
below the caves.

Paisley turned to Posso and Kelty.
"Now . . . let's go ashore and look
for the treasure." He looked up at
Spott in the crow's-nest.
"The whales are still
around, Spott, so you
stay here and keep
an eye out for
whale hunters."

"Aye, aye, cap'n,"
replied Spott.

33

Once ashore, Paisley pointed
upwards.

"There's a ledge there," he said.
"I bet that's where the treasure is."
"But how do we get up?" asked
Posso. "I can't see a way. It's too
steep."

Suddenly, Kelty cried out, "Over here! There's a tunnel that climbs into the mountain. Perhaps it will take us to the ledge."

"Let's go," said Paisley, and the three pirate penguins began to clamber up the steep slope.

"It's dark in here," said
Posso nervously.

"And smelly,"
added Kelty.

"That's because it's full of seaweed,"
answered Paisley, pulling his foot
out of the squelching, sticky mess.

"This stuff
is like
glue."

A few moments later they reached
the end of the tunnel and found
themselves at the entrance to the
twin caves.

Paisley laughed. "We're standing
inside the nostrils of Neptune!"
he said.

"Let's hope he doesn't sneeze again,"
muttered Posso anxiously.

Paisley peered over the edge.

"Yes!" he cried. "Down there on the ledge. There's a sea chest. It must be Grandpa's!"

Chapter Five

Carefully, Paisley climbed down to the ledge and attached a rope to the chest.

"Haul away!" he shouted.

Posso and Kelty gripped the rope
and slowly pulled the chest up to
the cave.

Paisley climbed
back up to
join them . . .

then they all took hold of the chest
and made their way down the tunnel
again.

Back on board the *Frozen Kipper*,
they placed the chest on the deck.

"Now . . ." said Paisley with a grin,
"let's see what's inside."

But just then Spott gave a shout.
"Whaler!"

Paisley, Posso and Kelty looked out
to sea and saw a big whaling ship
on the horizon. It was heading
straight for the whales.

Spott yelled out a warning. "Murkle!
Watch out! Whale hunters!"

Murkle and his friends heard the
shout and turned to escape.

But instead of
swimming into the
open sea, they panicked
and swam past the *Frozen
Kipper* into the narrow bay.

"Oh no!" cried Paisley in alarm.
"Now they're trapped!"

"What can we do?" said Posso
anxiously. "The whale hunters will
catch them."

Just then they heard a familiar
rumbling sound from the mountain.

"Hold on!" shouted
Paisley. "Neptune's
going to sneeze again!"

Everyone held on to something, and
a few moments later another huge
blast of air shot out of the caves.

SSCHOO!

This time bits of seaweed, disturbed by the penguins' feet, came blasting out too.

"Oi!" spluttered Spott as wet, sticky seaweed sprayed all over him. "What's going on?"

A slow smile spread over Paisley's face
as he looked up at the twin caves.

"That sneeze has
given me an
idea," he said.
"Not only will I
save the whales

but I'll make sure the whaling ship
can't chase them." He turned to Kelty.
"Quick," he said. "Fetch two shovels.
You and I are going ashore."

As Kelty climbed into the hold,
Paisley pointed to the wheel.
"While we're gone,
Posso, you turn the
ship so that it's
blocking the
entrance to
the bay."

Posso ran off to follow the order as
Kelty appeared with the shovels.

"Let's go!"
Paisley cried,
and they
sprang ashore.

Chapter Six

The big whaling ship sailed into the bay.

But it stopped when it saw that the *Frozen Kipper* was blocking its way to the whales.

"Hey!" the whaling master shouted
to Posso. "You there! Move that
lump of ice away and be quick
about it."

"I can't," replied Posso. "Not
without orders. I'm not the captain."
"Then who is?" bellowed the whaling
master.

"I am," called Paisley as he and
Kelty reappeared from the tunnel in
the mountain and clambered aboard
the *Frozen Kipper*.

"Then move your ship before I blast
it out of the water with my cannons!"
the whaling master yelled.

"In a moment . . ." said Paisley and
glanced upwards hopefully.

"No . . . now!" roared the whaling master.

"Yes . . . now!" shouted his crew, waving their horrible harpoons in the air. "We want to hunt those whales!"

Paisley anxiously looked up again at the twin caves and this time heard a faint rumble from inside the mountain.

He smiled and turned to the whaling master. "All right," he said, "we'll move."

Quickly, the *Frozen Kipper* sailed out of the way, and the whaling ship surged forward.

Just as it was passing under the nostrils of Neptune, another sneeze came roaring out.

But this time, instead of just a few
bits of seaweed appearing . . . out
came a huge torrent.

SSSCHOO!

All the seaweed that Paisley and
Kelty had piled up inside the nostrils
of Neptune came flying out!

In an instant, the whaling ship was covered. The green, smelly, sticky seaweed clung to the sails, stuck to the masts and deck, and covered the crew from head to foot.

The whaling ship was stopped in its tracks. Its master and crew could hardly move.

The pirate penguins laughed in delight.

"It'll take them ages to clean that stuff off," chortled Paisley. "They'll  be stuck here for days."

Murkle and his friends saw what had happened. Gratefully, they swam past the two ships and out of the bay.

"Thank you, Paisley," Murkle called in his slow, deep voice. "Thank you for keeping your promise."

Paisley and his crew waved goodbye, and the iceberg ship turned and followed the four whales into the open sea.

Chapter Seven

That night, far away from the
island of Neptune and the wild
Ice Wind, the *Frozen Kipper* dropped
anchor.

"Now," said Paisley, "let's have a
look at Grandpa Elgin's treasure."

56

He opened the rusty lid and the pirate penguins gathered round eagerly. Inside the chest were a fiddle, a flute, a trumpet and a concertina.

"Where's the treasure?" chorused Posso, Kelty and Spott, disappointed.

But Paisley grinned. "This is it," he said happily. "I told you my grandpa loved music. His musical instruments were his treasure."

Paisley lifted out the concertina and
gave it a squeeze.

"I hope you play the concertina
better than you sing," said Posso.

"I do,"
answered
Paisley.

"As well as your grandpa?"
asked Kelty.

Paisley smiled. He began to play
and a tuneful, lilting melody filled
the night air.

Then the pirate penguins heard
something else.
From far off, across the starlit ocean,
a wonderful, low, musical sound
drifted towards them.

Smiles grew on the faces of the crew.
"Listen," Posso whispered, enchanted.
"Paisley really can play as well as
his grandpa . . .

"The whales are singing!"